Another Point of View

BRAINY BIRD
SAVES THE DAY!

Library of Congress Cataloging-in -Publication Data

Granowsky, Alvin, 1936–
   Brainy bird saves the day! / by Alvin Granowsky ; illustrations by Eva Vagreti Cockrille.
Henny Penny / retold by Alvin Granowsky ; illustrations by Mike Krone.
      p. cm. — (Another point of view)
   Titles from separate title pages; works issued back-to-back and inverted.
   Summary: Juxtaposes the traditional tale of Henny Penny and her friends with a retelling in which the animals' more careful analysis of the situation helps them avoid a sad ending.
   ISBN 0-8114-7125-X — ISBN 0-8114-6632-9 (pbk.)
   1. Upside-down books—Specimens. [1. Folklore. 2. Upside-down books. 3. Toy and movable books.] I. Vagreti Cockrille, Eva, ill. II. Krone, Mike, ill. III. Granowsky, Alvin, 1936– Henny Penny. 1996. IV. Title. V. Series.
PZ8.1.G735Br   1996
398.2—dc20   95-9606
[E]   CIP
                                               AC

Printed and bound in the United States of America
  2 3 4 5 6 7 8 9 00 LB 00 99 98 97 96

BRAINY BIRD SAVES THE DAY!

by Dr. Alvin Granowsky
illustrations by Éva Vágréti Cockrille

STECK-VAUGHN
COMPANY

ELEMENTARY • SECONDARY • ADULT • LIBRARY

2

The sky is falling! The sky is falling! Who would say such a foolish thing? I wouldn't. I'm a bird brain, you know.

Do you think having a bird brain means being empty-headed? Well, it doesn't! But I know why you might think so. You've heard some silly tales about birds—especially about me!

Those tales are so silly! I can't believe
anyone would believe such silly tales.

Do you know what I think? I think those who
tell them are silly themselves!

4

An acorn did fall upon my head. Indeed, it did. When I looked up, I saw hundreds more ready to fall on other poor birds. As the king's reporter, it was my job to tell him about this danger. I had to hurry before other birds were hurt as I had been.

As I rushed to the king's palace, I came across Cocky Locky and Ducky Lucky.

"Where are you going in such a rush, Henny Penny?" asked Cocky Locky.

"Is there big news?" asked Ducky Lucky. "There must be a reason for you to be rushing off like this."

"Indeed there is!" I replied. "Just look at the bump on my head! There's a story behind it."

"Why, that bump is as big as an acorn!" Cocky Locky said. "Were you hit by a falling acorn?"

"Indeed I was," I replied. "You used your wonderful bird brain to figure that out, didn't you?"

"You must be going to report this to the king," Ducky Lucky said. "After all, where there is an acorn, there is an oak tree. And that tree must have hundreds of acorns about to drop on other birds' heads!"

"You are exactly right!" I said to Ducky Lucky. "You are truly a bird brain."

"We will join you in telling the king," said Cocky Locky.

"Yes," said Ducky Lucky. "The king must be told before all the barnyard birds have big bumps on their heads."

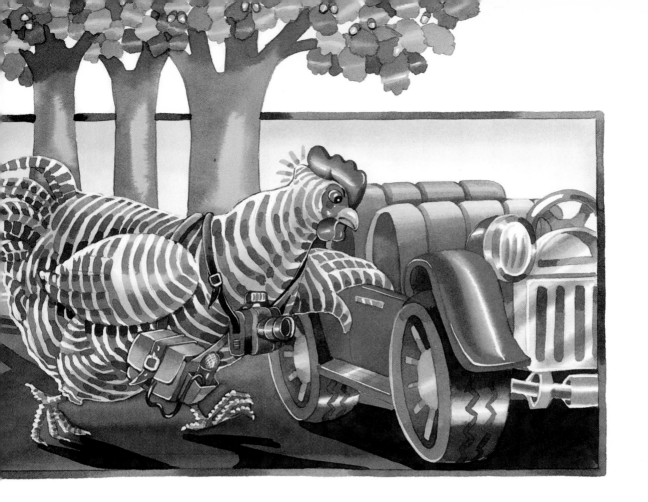

"We can open the bank a little later," said Cocky Locky.

"Yes," said Ducky Lucky. "Let's hurry and tell the king."

So we rushed off to tell the king that acorns were falling from the oak tree.

Then we found Goosey Loosey and Turkey Lurkey. I told them about the acorns and the need to tell the story.

"We will join you," said Goosey Loosey. "It is most important that the king hear of this danger at once!"

Turkey Lurkey said, "We have a patient with
brand new chicks. But the chicks are just fine,
and we can check on them again later today.
Right now the king must be told of the danger
from falling acorns!"

14

On the way to the palace, we came across
Foxy Loxy. "Where are you going in such a
rush?" he asked.

"We are going to tell the king about the
danger of falling acorns!" I said. I showed him
the big bump on my head. "This news must
be reported!"

"Of course you must tell the king!" said Foxy Loxy. "And you must hurry. I'll show you a short cut."

You didn't have to be a bird brain to know that Foxy Loxy was up to no good.

"Thank you so much for your help," said Ducky Lucky. "But do you mind telling us where that short cut leads? I think it goes to a cave."

"You are right!" said Foxy Loxy. "And do you know who lives in that cave?"

"Why no, we don't," we all replied.

"The king lives there," said Foxy Loxy. "He moved in just last week."

Did that silly fox think he could fool us that easily?

"Oh, dear me," I said. "I just remembered something I need for my story. We need to hurry back to the barnyard and get it. Tell the king we'll be right back."

What I needed for my story was to get rid of
that fox. And I knew just how to do it!

"Hurry, Fido!" I called for Farmer Brown's
great big hunting dog. "Come with us to see
Foxy Loxy." We all rushed back to the cave.

"Oh, Foxy Loxy," we called. "We have everything we need now. We're ready to see the king."

"Come right in," called Foxy Loxy. "The king is waiting!"

"**RUFF, RUFF, RUFF!**" barked Fido as he ran into Foxy Loxy's cave.

Foxy Loxy came racing out of the cave with Fido nipping at his bushy tail. We asked where the king was, but Foxy Loxy didn't answer.

We hurried to the king's palace and told him about the acorns. I got my story ready in time for that day's news. Because I warned everyone about the danger, the kingdom was safe again!

Now you know what really happened. So, who do you suppose is spreading that silly tale about my saying the sky was falling? Do you think it may be a fellow with a pointy nose and a bushy tail? Could it be someone who didn't get what he wanted for dinner? I wouldn't be a bit surprised. Would you?

From that day to this, no one has seen Henny Penny, Cocky Locky, Ducky Lucky, Goosey Loosey, or Turkey Lurkey again.

Do you know what else? The king has never been told that the sky is falling!

Another Point of View

Henny Penny

retold by Dr. Alvin Granowsky
illustrations by Mike Krone

STECK-VAUGHN
C O M P A N Y
ELEMENTARY • SECONDARY • ADULT • LIBRARY

2

nce upon a time, Henny Penny was eating in the barnyard when an acorn fell from a tree and **bopped** her on the head.

"Oh dear! This is terrible!" clucked Henny Penny. "The sky is falling. I must go tell the king."

So the upset hen dashed along the path to the palace until she met Cocky Locky.

"Cock-a-doodle-doo!" crowed Cocky Locky. "Where are you going in such a rush?"

"Oh, this is terrible!" clucked Henny Penny. "The sky is falling, and I am going to tell the king!"

4

"What? The sky is falling?" Cocky Locky
was shocked. "How do you know?"

"Well, a big piece of sky fell down and
bopped me right on the head," clucked
Henny Penny. "Just look at this bump!"

"Oh, that is terrible!" crowed Cocky Locky.
"The king must hear of this!"

So Henny Penny and Cocky Locky dashed
off to tell the king that the sky was falling.
The two birds ran along the path to the palace
until they met Ducky Lucky.

"Quack, quack, quack!" quacked Ducky
Lucky. "Where are you going in such a rush?"

"Oh, this is terrible!" said Henny Penny and
Cocky Locky. "The sky is falling, and we are
going to tell the king!"

7

"What? The sky is falling?" Ducky Lucky was shocked. "How do you know?"

"Well, a big piece of sky fell down and **bopped** me right on the head," clucked Henny Penny. "Just look at this bump!"

8

"Oh, that is terrible!" quacked Ducky Lucky. "The king must hear of this!"

So Henny Penny, Cocky Locky, and Ducky Lucky dashed off to tell the king that the sky was falling.

10

The three birds ran along the path to the palace until they met Goosey Loosey.

"Honk, honk, honk," honked Goosey Loosey. "Where are you going in such a rush?"

"Oh, this is terrible!" said the three birds. "The sky is falling, and we are going to tell the king!"

12

"What? The sky is falling?" Goosey Loosey was shocked. "How do you know?"

"Well, a big piece of sky fell down and **bopped** me right on the head," clucked Henny Penny. "Just look at this bump!"

"Oh, that is terrible!" honked Goosey Loosey. "The king must hear of this!"

So Henny Penny, Cocky Locky, Ducky
Lucky, and Goosey Loosey dashed off to tell
the king that the sky was falling. The four
birds ran along the path to the palace until
they met Turkey Lurkey.

14

"Gobble, gobble, gobble," gobbled Turkey
Lurkey. "Where are you going in such a rush?"

"Oh, this is terrible!" said Henny Penny,
Cocky Locky, Ducky Lucky, and Goosey Loosey.
"The sky is falling, and we are going to tell
the king!"

15

"What? The sky is falling?" Turkey Lurkey was shocked. "How do you know?"

"Well, a big piece of sky fell down and **bopped** me right on the head," clucked Henny Penny. "Just look at this bump!"

16

"Oh, that is terrible!" gobbled Turkey Lurkey. "The king must hear of this!"

So Henny Penny, Cocky Locky, Ducky Lucky, Goosey Loosey, and Turkey Lurkey dashed off to tell the king that the sky was falling. The five birds ran along the path to the palace until they met Foxy Loxy.

"Where are you going, Henny Penny, Cocky Locky, Ducky Lucky, Goosey Loosey, and Turkey Lurkey?" asked Foxy Loxy as he licked his lips.

"Oh, the sky is falling, and we are going to tell the king!" said the five birds.

"What? The sky is falling? How terrible!" said Foxy Loxy. "You must not waste a moment in telling the king!" The sly fox looked up at the blue sky and said, "Imagine what would happen if that sky fell down upon us all!"

"Oh, dear, dear, dear, dear, dear!" said the five upset birds. "That would be terrible! We must dash off to tell the king! We must not waste a moment!"

"Well, then, follow me," said the tricky Foxy Loxy. "I know a short cut to the palace."

21

So all the birds followed Foxy Loxy up the
hill and into a cave. And do you know what?
It was no short cut. The cave was where
Foxy Loxy lived!